Backpack Kitty
goes to camp

by Mister Ed
art by Mickey Gill

📖 SCHOLASTIC

BACKPACK KITTY GOES TO CAMP
"An energetic, fun-loving young girl decides to share her activites
from Camp Bo Peep with her sleep-loving cat."

Written by Ed Masessa
Illustrated and Designed by Mickey Gill

Published by Tangerine Press, an imprint of
Scholastic Inc; 557 Broadway;
New York, NY 10012

10 9 8 7 6 5 4 3 2 1

ISBN 0-439-86236-1

Printed and bound in the USA

Backpack Kitty
goes to camp

Backpack Kitty loves to sleep.
LuLu loves to play.

LuLu goes to Camp Bo Peep,
Kitty sleeps all day.

LuLu's day is filled with fun.
Her friends are nice and sweet.

Backpack Kitty lies in the sun
And dreams of things to eat.

But LuLu misses Kitty
and wants to share her fun.
She makes a special card for her with
glitter, rocks, and gum.

LuLu cannot wait to see
the look on Kitty's face.

Kitty dreams of eating flowers
sitting in the vase.

Backpack Kitty listens
as Lulu makes her plan
to turn the yard into a camp
for Kitty, Ned, and Fran.

That night, as LuLu dreams
of Kitty going for a twirl,

Kitty's dreams are filled with things like
sunny spots to curl.

"Surprise," said LuLu.
"It's time to go to Backpack Kitty Camp!"

"We'll play some games and you will be the
all-time Kitty champ."

Backpack Kitty hits the ball.
LuLu gives a cheer.

She bops it with a BIP, BOP, POW
until it disappears.

Next is a race to see who's fastest –
Kitty, Fran, or Ned.
Kitty holds her tail up high
and runs full speed ahead.

Backpack Kitty
loves to paint the
pictures LuLu drew.
Step in red, step in blue–
come on Kitty, let's paint two!

Time to rest, time for tea.
Kitty, Ned, and Fran
makes three!

LuLu makes a treat for Kitty –
yellow, green, and red.
How pretty Kitty looks
with a hat upon her head.

It's getting late and Backpack Kitty
needs a little nap.

LuLu makes a bed for her,
but Kitty likes a lap.

LuLu and Kitty sleep and dream
about their busy day.
Backpack Kitty dreams of sleep.
LuLu dreams of play.